THE MOOSE OF EWENKI

By Gerelchimeg Blackcrane • Illustrated by Jiu Er • Translated by Helen Mixter

AN ALDANA LIBROS BOOK

GREYSTONE KIDS

GREYSTONE BOOKS • VANCOUVER/BERKELEY

The Reindeer Ewenki people live in the vast forests of the Greater Hinggan Mountains in northern China. They hunt and raise reindeer.

On one of his hunting trips, the old hunter Gree Shek lay in ambush all night long. He shot a moose.

Gree Shek sat down to rest when he suddenly heard something rustling in the shrub behind him.

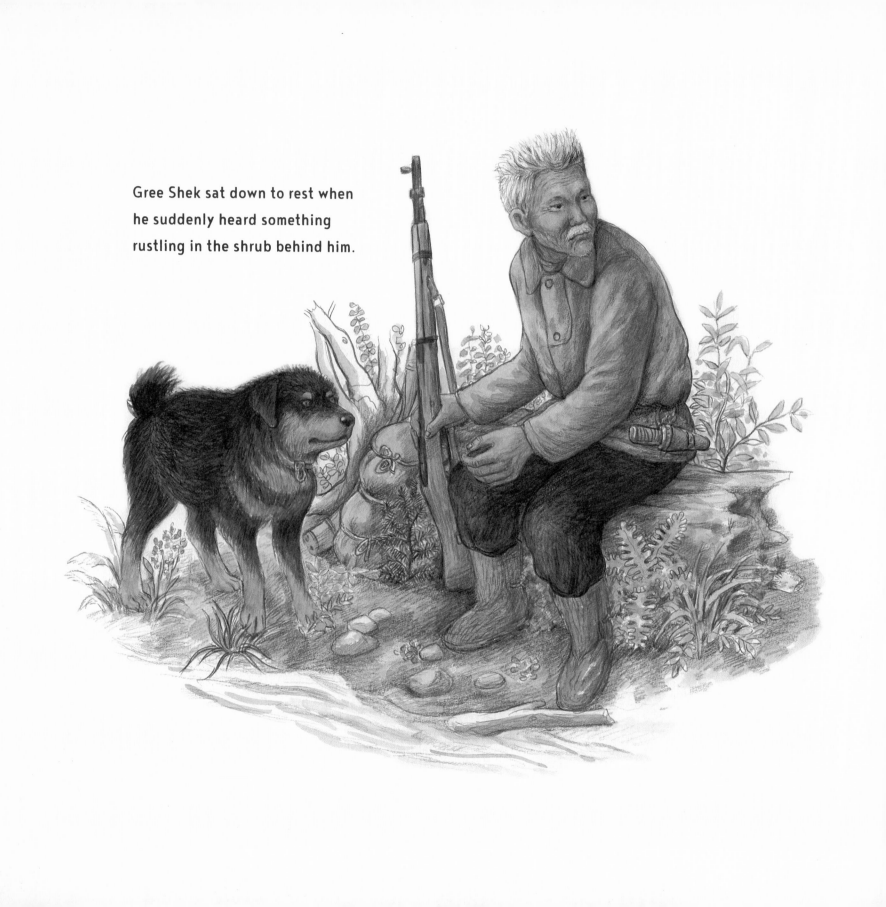

A baby animal looked out, trembling with fear. With its fiery fur, the little thing looked like the rising sun over the mountains. Gree Shek realized that it was a little moose!

The hunting dog barked and
growled, but Gree Shek told him
to be quiet and held him back.

Slowly, the little moose
came over and licked
Gree Shek's fingers.

The old man felt terrible because Reindeer Ewenki hunters would never
hunt a female moose who was raising a baby. When he had shot her,
he hadn't seen the baby moose lurking in the shrub. And it wasn't the
normal season for babies.

The motherless baby followed Gree Shek all the way back to the campsite.

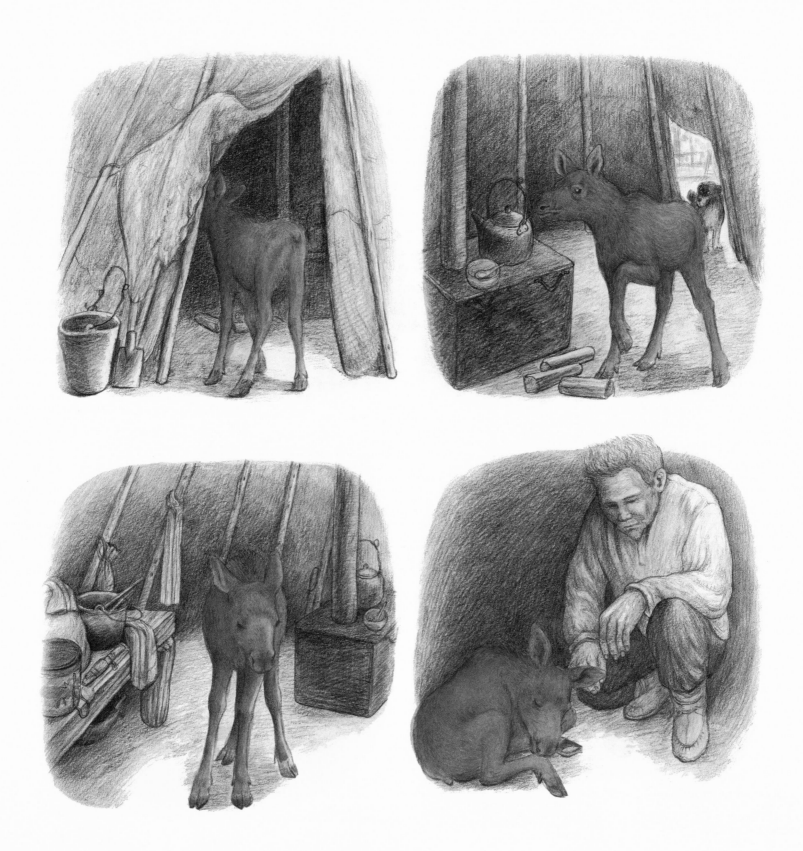

He was not afraid of people. He followed Gree Shek into his tent
and fell asleep in no time, beside the stove.

Exhausted, Gree Shek also fell sound asleep and escaped into his
dreams. He was awakened by a sudden bang—the little moose
had knocked down the food shelf.

The little moose was so hungry that he was searching for food all around the tent. Gree Shek found a bottle of reindeer milk. He rarely used it unless he wanted some milk for his tea, and it had almost fermented into chunks by now. But he dipped a finger into the bottle and fed the little moose. Quickly, the baby licked it all up.

But he was still hungry. He stumbled around the dark tent looking for something to eat. The rice and flour were soon gone. He even tried to eat the candle.

And he kept Gree Shek awake the whole night.

The next day, the little moose began
his new life at the campsite. He learned
to drink reindeer milk and eat rice,
and even grew fond of bread. He liked
all kinds of human food in his belly,
and he never seemed to be full.

Gree Shek named him Xiao Han, which means Little Moose.

Xiao Han grew and grew, and before long,
he was as big as an adult reindeer.

But he didn't seem to know how big he was. He played outside all
day long, but still came into the tent to sleep. Xiao Han couldn't even
turn around in there, so one day, he knocked the whole thing down.
Gree Shek had no choice but to kick him out.

Xiao Han followed Gree Shek around everywhere,
all day long. He was curious about everything.

At the campsite at night, he slept with the reindeer, all huddled together on the ground. Gree Shek lit a fire and burned incense to keep away the mosquitoes that tormented the animals.

As he grew older, Xiao Han went into the forest
with the reindeer to search for something to eat.
Living with the reindeer pack, he thought that
he was a reindeer, too.

When summer came, Xiao Han began to look for food in streams and ponds.
He ate water lilies, cattails, and duckweed.

Gree Shek kept on calling him Xiao Han, Little Moose, even when he had grown into a giant.

In the season when the reindeer were competing for females with whom to mate, the male reindeer began to challenge Xiao Han to fight. But he was so strong that he won every struggle.

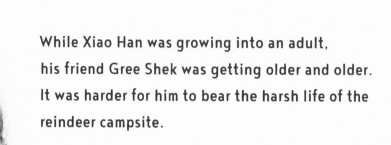

While Xiao Han was growing into an adult,
his friend Gree Shek was getting older and older.
It was harder for him to bear the harsh life of the
reindeer campsite.

One autumn, he sprained his foot while
he was out searching for the herd.

Gree Shek's foot had to be treated in the Aoluguya village at the bottom
of the mountain. Xiao Han, who had never left Gree Shek's side, followed
him all the way down to the settlement.

Gree Shek had to lock Xiao Han up in the courtyard. But there was nothing for him to do there. He was used to life in the wild. One day, he pushed through the fence.

The village dogs went crazy at the sight of him. For the dogs, moose were wild animals that had been hunted by the Reindeer Ewenki people for generations.

But now, suddenly, here was a moose in their village! So, they attacked him.

But Xiao Han was a giant and very powerful, though he didn't seem to know how strong he really was.

He tossed the dogs around like leaves blown by a crazy wind.

The human world was full
of temptations for Xiao Han.

He pushed into an unlocked warehouse and stole many, many bean cakes and drank a great deal of water. The bean cakes swelled in his belly until it looked like a drum.

Gree Shek led Xiao Han around all night long.
At dawn, with a huge PLOP, Xiao Han finally
rid himself of the bean cakes.

The human world was also filled with danger for Xiao Han.

Some in the Aoluguya village wanted to kidnap him and sell him to the zoo in the nearby city. They lured him into a noose using carrots. But Xiao Han was so strong that he knocked all the kidnappers down and almost tipped their truck over, before coming home to Gree Shek.

Gree Shek knew in his heart that Xiao Han would never get used to the human world in the village. So he brought him back up the mountain to the reindeer campsite.

But Gree Shek was growing weaker and weaker.

One morning, he took Xiao Han into the wildest part of the forest.

He tried to drive Xiao Han away by hitting and pushing him.
He tried everything he could think of, but Xiao Han wouldn't budge.

It had been six years since the morning when Gree Shek first brought
Xiao Han to the campsite. The moose had never left his side since then.

But now, Gree Shek had no choice other than to give him back to the
forest. Eventually, he shot at the ground beside Xiao Han. The stones
bounced up and hit Xiao Han on the nose.

In pain, Xiao Han finally ran off into the depths of the forest, leaving a sad Gree Shek behind. He returned alone to the reindeer camp that had emptied for the season.

On one late-autumn day, fierce winds rose up from all directions and blew the roofs off houses and tore up huge trees in the Aoluguya village.

Some young hunters from the village rushed up to the reindeer campsite on the mountain to see how Gree Shek was faring, only to find that he had been dead for a long time.

They buried Gree Shek on the high slope in hopes that his soul would go with the wind. His hunting dog insisted on staying behind to guard his master.

The young hunters drove the pack of reindeer away from the campsite and never set foot in that part of the forest again.

Years later, a poacher crept into the forest, hoping to hunt some wild reindeer. He saw the towering shadow of a giant moose far in the distance. He was so frightened that he shot all the bullets in his gun at the moose. But they missed. The moose rushed at him and, tossing his antlers, threw him far away into the bush.

From then on, no one ever dared to enter that forest again.

The Reindeer Ewenki people still tell each other that up on the mountain, there lives a giant moose. He is guarding the vast forest and Gree Shek, his dead hunter.